JUNGLE DOCTOR'S MONKEY TALES

②

JUNGLE DOCTOR'S MONKEY TALES

Paul White

CF4·K

10 9 8 7 6 5 4 3 2 1

Jungle Doctor's Monkey Tales ISBN 978-1-84550-609-4

© Copyright 1957 Paul White

First published 1957. Reprinted six times.
Paperback edition 1972. Reprinted twice. Revised 1984,
Reprinted 1986, 1988, 1990, 1995

Published in 2010 by
Christian Focus Publications, Geanies House, Fearn, Tain
Ross-shire, IV20 1TW, Scotland, U.K.
Paul White Productions,
4/1-5 Busaco Road, Marsfield, NSW 2122, Australia

Cover design: Daniel van Straaten
Cover illustration: Andy Robb
Interior illustrations: Graham Wade
Printed and bound by Bell and Bain, Glasgow

Mixed Sources
Product group from well-managed
forests and other controlled sources
www.fsc.org Cert no. TT-COC-002769
© 1996 Forest Stewardship Council
FSC

Scripture quotations are either the author's own paraphrase
or are taken from The New Testament in Modern English,
copyright © 1958, 1959, 1960
J.B. Phillips and 1947, 1952, 1955, 1957
The Macmillian Company, New York.
Used by permission. All rights reserved.

CONTENTS

INTRODUCTION 7

PROLOGUE.. 9

1. THE GOAT WHO WANTED TO BECOME A LION 11

2. BEWARE OF PUMPKINS 21

3. OUT ON A LIMB... 27

4. NYANI AND THE MATTER OF EGGS 35

5. THE CATCH IN CAMOUFLAGE.. 43

6. TOTO CROSSES THE EQUATOR.. 51

7. MONKEYS FIND SOLID SAFETY 59

8. FAMOUS MONKEY LAST WORDS.. 67

9. THE MEDICALLY-MINDED MONKEY 75

GLOSSARY 85

SAMPLE CHAPTER.. 87

INTRODUCTION

Paul White learned a great deal from his African friends at the jungle hospital. They befriended him and helped him in his efforts to learn their language, Chigogo.

One of their most important gifts was to teach him how to use animal stories. These stories, or fables, helped to explain abstract thoughts and theological terms.

When the Whites were on their way home from Africa in 1941, they were delayed in Colombo because of German submarine activity. Paul was invited to speak at a girls' boarding school. All the children of non-Christian faiths were sent outside but, hearing laughter from inside, crowded round the windows to see what they were missing. This was the first of many occasions when audiences were gripped by the fable stories.

The first of six fable books appeared in 1955. A menagerie of African animals is used to teach the gospel and how to live the Christian life. In these books you will meet Toto, the mischievous monkey, Boohoo, the hippo who, like the author, suffered from allergies, Twiga, the giraffe and wise teacher, and many others.

They will endear themselves to you as they have to thousands round the globe.

PROLOGUE

'Dogs are animals of great understanding,' said Daudi.

Mgogo agreed. How often had he wished with strength for a dog of his own!

Daudi's voice broke into his thoughts.

'Behold, Chibwa has become the father of pups; this is the smallest.'

Mgogo stroked the little animal. '*Hongo*, Great One, it is a creature of joy.'

Jungle Doctor's assistant picked up the puppy and put it into the African boy's hands.

Daudi smiled. 'It is a gift; he is yours. Look after him with care, for he is newborn and of small strength.'

'*Kah!*' gasped the delighted Mgogo. '*Assante Muwaha*, thank you, Great One. I will follow your words and will bring him with me to the campfire at the time of telling stories.'

The small dog licked his hand.

Mgogo beamed. 'Truly, he is an animal of joy.'

Daudi nodded. 'He will fill your days with work and open your eyes to many new things.'

1

THE GOAT WHO WANTED TO BECOME A LION

It was an hour after sunset at the hospital. Daudi, Jungle Doctor's assistant, looked at the intent faces of those who listened. He smiled as he saw Mgogo sitting on a pumpkin nursing his small dog.

'My story is of a goat who was very strong indeed. Your eyes told you of his strength and so did your nose.' There was a ripple of laughter in the firelight.

Mbuzi, the goat, tossed his head and remarked to his shadow, 'I am a goat of strength – a splendid creature. It isn't right for such a distinguished animal to remain a mere goat.'

Thoughts rambled through his goaty mind and after a time an idea grew in his small brain. In his loud and unmusical voice he told the jungle, 'I shall become a lion!' But nobody took any notice. They were used to the ways and the words of goat. So he pranced along to the *buyu* tree where Nyani, the monkey, sat in the sun happily eating cockroaches.

Mbuzi stopped. 'Oh, monkey of wisdom,' he brayed. 'I wish above all things to become a lion. Tell me. How do goats become lions?'

Monkey hung by his tail. This always helped him to think better. He chattered and frowned and mumbled impressively and then swung himself onto a suitable branch. He cleared his throat and said in an important voice, 'For goats to become lions, behold, there are four rules. First, they must *go* where lions *go*.' He paused and impressively lifted the second monkey finger. 'They must *do* what lions *do*.'

Goat nodded eagerly. Monkey put his head on one side. 'Thirdly, goats who wish to become lions must *say* what lions *say*.' Nyani took up a dramatic pose and waved his fourth finger. 'Finally, you must *eat* what lions *eat*. Do all these things and you will become a lion.'

Goat's eyes rolled as he tried to concentrate. 'GO where lions go,' he muttered. 'DO …' – the words were lost in a mumble. 'SAY …' – his voice became a trial roar that ended shrilly. He stopped uncertainly, goat memory failing. But Monkey was ready. ' … and EAT what lions eat,' he prompted.

With a *M-a-a-a* of triumph Mbuzi set out, his goat legs moving in as lion-like a way as he could make them. His tail was harder to manage for a goat's tail is a restless thing. Then with a tremendous effort he controlled it and stalked sedately down the middle of the road.

In the shade of a boulder he stopped and spent some time in roaring practice. His discouragement

when his roar changed to a squeak was forgotten on seeing a large bone. Eagerly he picked this up and began to gnaw and roar and roar and gnaw. He was so pleased with the result that he put the bone carefully under his left leg and recited:

'GO and DO and SAY and EAT.'

As each foot sedately touched the road (he now moved down the exact middle) he said in a new deep tone, 'Go where the lions go, do what lions do, say what lions say and eat what lions eat.'

Mbuzi stopped. He felt that someone was watching him. With a small smile he thought, 'Ah, I meet a fellow lion.'

At that moment a long shadow stretched down the road. Goat adjusted his tail, gnawed his bone and moved forward again, his muscles rippling. From his great height Twiga, the giraffe, smiled down. 'The sun has strength these days, Mbuzi.'

Goat roared and waved his bone in a menacing way. 'I am a lion. I'm going to eat you, Twiga.'

'Yes. Yes.' Twiga's voice was soothing. 'I understand. Now be a wise goat, go home, take two paw-paw leaves, place them on each side of your head and rest it on a cool stone. You'll feel better tomorrow.'

Misery filled goat's voice. 'I'm a lion, a *lion*, a LION ...'

Giraffe nodded his head kindly and walked off into the shade. With legs and tail behaving very much like any other goat and with tears running down his beard, Mbuzi rushed back to the *buyu* tree. 'Monkey,' he bleated, 'it hasn't happened. I have no joy. I've done and said and eaten and gone and behold I am still a goat.'

Nyani considered the problem but, as everyone knows, monkey brains move slowly. 'How stupid of me! Of course it didn't work.'

Goat pranced about impatiently, 'What else must I do?'

But Monkey was too busy to talk. He tore up a piece of bark from a tree, picked up a lump of charcoal and sat on a smooth rock and worked with great care.

Goat peered over his shoulder and saw strange marks which to him looked like the word L-I-O-N. 'Wear this,' chortled Monkey, making a hole in the bark with his finger and then pulling it over the shorter of Mbuzi's horns. 'There.' He stood back admiring his work. 'You're labelled. Every educated creature in the jungle will now know that you're a lion.'

A warm feeling of joy crept through Goat and he barely heard Monkey say, 'And any gift you might like to leave under this *buyu* tree would be appreciated.'

Thinking lion-like thoughts, Mbuzi strode through the jungle, his tail moving to and fro, his prancing exactly like that of the king of the beasts, his bleat growing more of a roar with every step while the way he gnawed the bone was all that could be asked of any lion. 'Go and eat and do and say,' he muttered to himself. His eyes gleamed as he saw a movement in the shadow. Here was one of his new species. He stepped forward but mild disgust wrinkled his nose when he saw that the animal coming down the road towards him was Zebra.

The striped-one stopped and looked at him rather anxiously. Goat gnawed and roared in what he felt was the best lion tradition. Zebra smiled. 'The sun's very hot these days, Mbuzi. Do you think it is wise for you to go out in the middle of the day?'

In as deep a voice as he could manage Goat said, 'I shall eat you if you're not very careful and respectful. Do you not see that I have become a lion?' He shook his label under Zebra's nose. 'I go where lions go. I do what lions do. I eat what lions eat and I say what lions say.'

Zebra nodded. 'Of course you do. But now go home and wrap your head in paw-paw leaves and rest it on a nice cool stone and you'll feel ...'

Goat's tail twitched most goatily and he rushed down the road in a rage, his label flying in the wind. Zebra looked after him and laughed till his stripes became tangled.

On walked Mbuzi towards the place where lions lived, roaring loudly. He strode round a great rock. It was a place of echoes and his loud voice reverberated especially in a shaded cavern. Goat adjusted his label and carefully went through his routine. 'Is there a lion in the house?' His voice was unnaturally deep. 'Is there a lion in the house?' replied the echo.

Mbuzi felt his hide creep and goose pimples appeared in his more delicate sections. 'Is there a LION?' he roared, and his ears were charmed by the way the echoes treated his voice. But he was startled as the volume of sound grew and grew when his lips had long been silent.

In the tawny sunlight a large shadow moved. Then came Mbuzi's voice again, slightly high-pitched. 'I have become a lion,' he stopped suddenly seeing a great tail moving majestically. A singularly unbrotherly feeling gripped him as hot, hungry breath swept into his face and huge paws hurled at him striking off his label.

The cavern overflowed with thunderous noises which slowly changed to the ominous crack of bones and the chomping of great jaws hard at work.

Goat had become ...

Daudi hesitated. Mgogo's eager voice broke in. '… had become a lion's dinner.'

'Truly, and there's only one way that a goat could become a lion.' There was a pause and a voice replied, 'The only way would be for goat to be born a second time as a lion cub.'

Daudi leant forward. 'Right. That's just it. These are the words of Jesus himself. "You must be born again." It isn't what you do or say or where you go or what you eat that makes you a Christian. Jesus is the only one who can do that. He died. Men crucified him. But he came back to life to make it clear to us that he is God. He came to earth not to produce better men of the old kind but a new kind of men and he does this so willingly when you come to him and ask him to forgive your sins and to make you one of his family.'

Those that listened sat quietly. Then Mboga smiled. 'There is small profit in following the combined wisdom of Goat and Monkey.'

* * *

What's Inside the Fable?

Special Message: Nobody can join or even understand the Kingdom of God without being born again.

Jesus told about it. *John chapter 3 verses 3 to 17.*

Paul summed it up. *Titus chapter 3 verses 3 to 8.*

2
BEWARE OF PUMPKINS

'The less a trap looks like a trap the better the chance of it working,' laughed Daudi as he and Mgogo walked to the campfire.

'Nobody is really scared of a pumpkin – not even monkeys. This one was a splendid trap.'

Chuma, the leopard hunter, walked through his garden and stopped. He looked amongst the great leaves of a plant with yellow flowers and said, 'That is the largest pumpkin I have ever grown. It will make a splendid trap for monkeys who in turn will become the bait in my leopard trap.'

He set to work with his hunting knife, cut out the stalk and carefully made a hole just big enough to let him scoop out a lot of the pumpkin seeds. With care he removed much of the yellow inside the pumpkin. Then he poured in sand and covered this with many peanuts, putting the pumpkin on the path near a

big *buyu* tree. He walked over towards the place of monkeys, throwing peanuts in such a way that they would make a trail right up to the trap.

He thought, 'Monkey eyes will see those nuts or monkey noses will smell them. They will follow the peanuts greedily and then they'll find the pumpkin.' He chuckled and went and sat in the shade behind the big *buyu* tree.

There were many monkeys looking for acacia pods. The largest and greediest of them was Tumbo.

A small, nimble monkey scrambled down the tree and ran along the path chattering and picking up peanut after peanut. Others followed him. Tumbo could not run as fast as the others. When they all came to the pumpkin they ate the peanuts they could see but when Tumbo appeared he pushed the others aside. He came to the pumpkin. It was rich with the smell of peanuts. He peered through the hole

but could see nothing. He put
his nose to it and smelled. *Ah!*
How good it was. His monkey
mind told him, 'All you
have to do is put your
paw through that hole
and the peanuts are
yours – all of them.'
He didn't hesitate.
His paw shot through
the hole and grabbed
all the peanuts he could
hold. He pulled it back quickly but
it stopped suddenly and painfully at the wrist. The
grasped peanuts in that paw would not let it come
through the hole in the huge pumpkin.

Tumbo squealed and the
other members of his tribe
chattered and squeaked
as well, and gave much
monkey advice. Tumbo did
everything he knew to pull
his paw out but it would
not come.

Twiga, the giraffe, peered
over a thornbush. 'Let go
the peanuts, Monkey,' he
advised kindly, 'and then
your paw will come out.'

But it is not the habit
of monkeys to let go.

Twiga's voice came louder. 'It's the peanuts that trap you. Let them go and you'll be free.'

The hunter moved out from behind the *buyu* tree.

All the other monkeys bolted into the treetops. Tumbo was frightened. He dragged the pumpkin some distance up the path but still his paw would not come out.

'Let go the nuts and you're safe,' again called Twiga.

But such is the wisdom of monkeys that they do not let go what they hold. The hunter walked towards him up the path, grabbed Tumbo by the back of his neck, split the pumpkin open with his knife and put Monkey, still grasping the nuts, into a bag and tied string round the top.

Tumbo had been trapped, for he had followed his way of monkey wisdom.

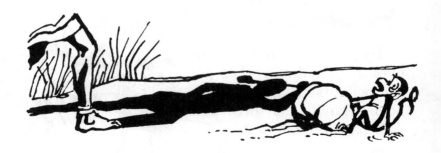

From underneath his three-legged stool Daudi produced a bag of peanuts and shared them with those that listened. As the shells were thrown onto the campfire, small flames lit up the faces of those who had heard the story.

'Well,' asked Daudi, 'what is the name of the trap?'

There was a lot of whispering and several voices said, 'It is sin.'

Daudi nodded. 'You're right. It's only a matter of monkey wisdom to think that you can get away from this trap if you cling to the things which take away your freedom and bring death.'

The voice of Hyena came eerily on the African night air.

Mgogo whispered to his small dog, 'There are many who laugh at sin, but, behold, it is a deadly thing.'

* * *

What's Inside the Fable?

Special Message: Sin is your worst enemy – your greatest danger.

Read what Paul writes: *Romans chapter 5 verses 12 to 19 and chapter 6 verses 5 to 23.*

God treats sin seriously. The story of the Flood makes this clear. *Genesis chapter 6 verse 5 to chapter 8 verse 22.*

3
OUT ON A LIMB

Mboga, who was Daudi's special assistant, loved to laugh but that day he had a problem and his face showed it. 'Bwana Daudi, as I read the Bible I find many words of difficulty, words that make my brain stumble.'

'What words?'

Mboga turned over the pages of a worn book. 'It says, "Repent, then, and turn to God, so that your sins may be wiped out".'

'Tonight,' said Daudi, 'I'll tell you a story that will help you to understand both those hard words.'

After sunset they settled round the fire and he kept his promise.

Under the buyu tree that grew on the edge of the deep, dark ravine, Moto and many of his small relations stared wide-eyed as their Uncle Nyani sharpened his great jungle knife – *panga* – on a smooth, flat stone.

He paused to test its edge on the hairs of his tail and growled. 'There is no *panga* like my *panga*.' He swung it in the air and shouted to the small ones who watched, 'Don't ever touch my *panga*. If any of you puts even the tip of his tail on it then he will feel the flat of it in the place where his hair is least. Do you hear me?'

But later on when the sun was hot, Nyani stretched out in the shade of his favourite limb and snoozed. Moto's eyes told him that his uncle was asleep and when his ears reported the sound of monkey snoring he crept up to the sharpening stone. How the edge of that great knife shone! How sharp and strong was the blade! How smooth and polished was the handle! His eyes sparkled. He touched *panga* with his paw. Truly the handle was as smooth as it looked. His tail curled gently round that handle and *yoh!* a thrill passed through his body. His tail tightened and quite by accident the blade rang against the stone.

With a roar Nyani leapt down, grabbed Moto and put him across his knee. 'I told you not to touch my *panga.*' *Wallop!*

'*Yow!*' yelled Moto. How he hated his monkey uncle's hard paw.

'If ever you put even the tip of your finger on it again I'll ...' WALLOP!

'*Ouch!*' yelled Moto. How he hated his monkey uncle's loud voice.

'You keep away from my part of the family tree, Moto. Do you hear me?' WALLOP!

'*Wow!*' yelled Small Monkey. How he hated his uncle's favourite limb!

Making sounds of no joy he limped to the ground nursing his resentment. Hyena came out of the shadows and sniggered, 'Hurt, didn't it? If he was my uncle I know what I'd do.'

Moto's tail tingled as he listened to Hyena's scheme of how to get his own back on Uncle Nyani. At last the day came when Nyani went over the hill to consult with other senior monkeys. Moto looked this way and that and saw no one. He rubbed the spot where his uncle's paw had hit so hard.

He knew exactly what he would do. How often he had dreamed of holding *panga* in his paws and chopping off Nyani's favourite limb which stretched far out over the ravine. As he gazed at *panga* he could almost see chips flying, hundreds of chips. Taking a deep breath he grasped the polished handle 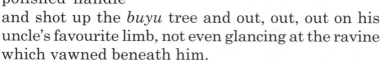 and shot up the *buyu* tree and out, out, out on his uncle's favourite limb, not even glancing at the ravine which yawned beneath him.

A delicious thrill ran up his spine as he swished the sharp blade through the air.

'Beautiful,' gloated Moto. He spat on his paws, swung *panga* back and WHAM!

Twiga, the giraffe, and Suku, the parrot, were under the umbrella tree. They blinked with amazement as they saw Small Monkey halfway out on his uncle's limb shouting at the top of his voice and wildly swinging *panga*.

'Look at him,' screeched Suku. 'Look what he's doing. Look where he's doing it!'

Twiga set off at a gallop. 'Moto, stop chopping,' he called. 'Danger!'

But Moto didn't listen. His laughter echoed back from the depths below. 'Won't Uncle be furious? His favourite limb gone, cut off with his *panga*.' Chips flew. Monkey grinned and chopped and puffed.

Twiga came as close as he could. 'Moto, it's only monkey wisdom to chip where you're chopping, to do what you're doing.'

But Moto could only think of flying chips and revenge and angry uncles.

Suku flew above Monkey's head. 'When your uncle finds his limb gone, what then?'

Moto grinned. 'He won't find me. As soon as it's off so am I.'

Suku swooped down into the shadow. 'You can say that again.'

Giraffe stretched out his long neck. 'It's the worst sort of monkey wisdom to be out on a limb and do what you're doing. Think, Monkey, think! Go to the safe side, the trunk side.' But his only answer was a shower of chips.

Suku fluttered round Twiga's head. 'Doesn't he see what must happen – what *will* happen? Try again, Twiga.'

'Monkey, Moto Monkey,' called Giraffe. 'Change your mind about where you're standing. Change over to the safe side.'

From below Mbisi, the hyena, sneered, 'Wonderful thing – monkey wisdom.'

Vibi, the vulture, nodded his scrawny neck. 'But useful for us. Dinner's nearly ready.'

Moto stopped for a short rest. Suku flew over and perched opposite him. 'Listen, stupid. Change your mind about where you're standing then follow your mind with your feet over to safety.'

Monkey picked up *panga* threateningly. 'I know what I'm doing.'

'Of course you do,' giggled Hyena.

'Shut your beak, Parrot,' croaked Vulture. 'Let the little fellow have his fun. You do what you like, Moto. Teach that old monkey a lesson.'

Little Monkey puffed out his chest. *Pow!* The great knife flashed. The cut in the limb grew deeper.

Twiga's voice was shrill now. 'Change your mind quickly, fast as you can! Change your direction.'

Suddenly the limb creaked. Moto grinned. 'It won't be long now.'

WHAM! went *panga*. CRACK went the limb. 'Change your mind,' shrieked Suku.

'Change your direction!' yelled Giraffe.

Moto suddenly realized what was happening. *Panga* slipped from his clammy paws. The limb began to tilt. In panic Moto rushed further out on the sagging limb.

'The other way. Turn round. Change your direction!' yelled Twiga.

Moto hesitated – but such is monkey wisdom that he did nothing. With a final groaning C-R-A-C-K the limb broke. Down, down hurtled Monkey and limb to the very bottom of the deep, dark ravine.

'Eheh,' said Mboga. 'A story of small joy. Behold, monkey wisdom is a strange thing.'

'Eheh,' agreed a voice. 'If only he had changed his mind.'

'Ah,' said Daudi. 'Now you're understanding it. To repent means to change your mind about going your own sinful way and to start going God's way.

'Conversion means changing your direction – not just your mind but all of you, all you are and all you have.'

Eagerly Mboga nodded. 'If Monkey had changed his mind he would have repented. If he'd changed his direction that would be like conversion?'

'Truly,' said Daudi. 'And the safe side?'

Many voices from round the fire answered, ' … is God's side.'

* * *

What's Inside the Fable?

Special Message: Make a U-turn – Repent.

Read about Peter's adventure in *Acts chapter 3 verses 1 to 19.*

There's also the amazing story of the man who turned from being the enemy of all who followed Jesus to become a great Christian leader. *Acts chapter 9 verses 1 to 22.*

4
NYANI AND THE MATTER OF EGGS

Mboga loved laughter and riddles. He held up an egg. 'Bwana Daudi, Kookoo, the hen, laid this today. Tell me, how may a good egg become bad?'

'Yoh!' chuckled Daudi. 'That's simple. Just leave it and it will go bad by itself.'

Mboga grinned. 'But how may a bad egg become good?'

There was a ripple of laughter round the campfire. 'This does not happen,' said Mgogo.

Daudi leaned forward. 'Truly, in the matter of eggs it doesn't. But in the matter of men's lives it does. God knows what we're like inside. All are bad, for God's book says, "There is no one righteous. No, not one." But God, and only God, can change a bad person into a good person. That's why Jesus came.'

'Now listen to the story of Nyani and the eggs.'

Toto and his small monkey sister, Boko, were nearly always hungry. They would eat nuts and berries, fruit and beetles, hairy caterpillars and cockroaches. But above everything else they liked eggs.

They had climbed up a buyu tree and the crows who lived there fluttered angrily around, squawking and cawing and making a great fuss. Toto laughed. 'Where there are birds you find ...'

'Nests,' giggled Boko. 'And where you find nests you find eggs.'

Toto swung through the branches, saw a nest and came back clutching a rather grubby crow's egg. He threw it to Boko who caught it with difficulty and threw it back so carelessly that although Toto clutched with paws and tail he could not hold it.

The somewhat soiled egg fell with a sickly plop and broke on the limb below. The gooey, greenish stuff that dripped heavily to the ground brought joy to the flies but to no one else in that part of the jungle.

Holding their noses the little monkeys scampered off. Ahead of them they saw their Uncle Nyani walking down the path to the river. In his paw, held very daintily, was an egg still warm from the nest of Kookoo, the hen. He licked his lips. With great care he made a small hole in the egg, put it to his mouth and sucked with purpose and strength. He cheeks hollowed and his eyes stood out as he sucked.

The small monkeys watched him with envy. When the shell was completely empty Nyani threw it untidily to the ground – a well-known habit of some monkeys. He sighed contentedly. 'Eggs are a comfort and a joy to a monkey's stomach.' His tongue went all the way round his lips. 'that is, some eggs are – but certain eggs ...'

Nyani shook his finger at the small monkeys who listened open-mouthed. His voice gradually grew louder. 'Some eggs offend the nose. They're a sadness to the mouth and can be an insult to your inner monkey.'

Toto and Boko nodded in complete agreement. 'But how can you tell which eggs are which, oh monkey of great experience?'

Nyani nodded his head slowly. He held an imaginary egg between his thumb and his first finger. 'There are those who hold the egg between their eye and the sun. These are called those who look. But the sharpest eye of the wisest monkey may lead him astray. There are also those who listen.' Nyani held the imaginary egg to his egg to his ear and shook it. 'But the best of monkey ears may be deceived.' He leaned forward and spoke confidentially. 'There are those of smaller monkey wisdom who crack the shell and sniff.'

Two small monkey noses wrinkled and Toto asked, 'How does a monkey of experience like you deal with this problem?'

A crafty look spread over Elder Monkey's face. 'Long acquaintance with eggs has taught me to take a large gourd, fill it with water and place the egg in the water. Those that sink to the bottom are eggs of worth that will bring comfort and light to the eye and joy to the stomach.'

Nyani changed his position on the limb. A harsh note came into his voice. 'Eggs that neither float to the top nor sink to the bottom are fit only for gifts to those for whom you have but small respect.'

Boko shook her head sadly. She remembered how once she had delivered such a gift. Nyani's voice became shrill. 'But eggs that float to the top – I say it again – that float to the top – eggs of that sort, grip your nose with one paw and with the other throw them with skill in the same direction as the wind blows.'

Much monkey sadness was saved, for the words they heard that day found a place to live between the ears of both Toto and Boko.

Daudi smiled at all those who looked up at him. 'Because you cannot see through its shell you need to test an egg in water. But remember, God can see through you. He needs no gourd of water to know what you're thinking. Nothing can be hidden from him.'

* * *

What's Inside the Fable?

Special Message: You can't hide anything from God.

Read *1 Samuel chapter 16 verse 7*.

Joshua chapter 7 tells the tragedy of the man who thought he could disobey God and hide a treasure from him.

Jesus even knew what men were thinking. *Matthew chapter 9 verses 1 to 7*.

5

THE CATCH IN CAMOUFLAGE

Mgogo's small dog crept under Daudi's stool and curled up. The storyteller laughed. 'He thinks he's hidden. I want to tell you again that the most skilful cannot hide from God. Listen to the story of the chameleon, the wilful giraffe and the leopard.'

Lwivi, the chameleon, sat on a small branch of the umbrella tree and practised changing colours by moving from one spot to another. Twiga's most difficult nephew, Riff-raff, stood watching him as he turned brown and then green and then yellow.

Chameleon puffed out his chest and said in his squeaky voice, 'Turn your head, Small Giraffe, and count from one to a hundred. Behold, I can hide even from your sharp eyes.' He moved to a place where brown bark met green leaves and yellow flowers. He became brown and green and yellow in a moment.

Giraffe counted, 'Ninety-seven, ninety-eight, nine-nine, a hundred. Coming, ready or not.' He twitched his ears, wrinkled his nose and opening his eyelids wide looked here and there but at first saw no sign of Lwivi. Wrinkling his forehead he peered down branch after branch and there, absurdly close, was Chameleon, skilfully camouflaged and almost invisible.

Headstrong Giraffe was peeved with the small creature's skill. With a flick of his nose he shook the branch and Lwivi staggered, lost his grip, fell from high in the tree and landed upside down bruising not only his pride in the fall.

Riff-raff jeered. 'Chameleons can't hide from me. *But I am different.* With my yellow skin and brown spots I'm invisible beneath umbrella trees. The sunlight and the shadows are a wonderful hiding place, for my spots are shadow and my skin is sunlight. Even Chewi, the leopard, would not notice

me there. Truly, I am hidden even from the keenest eyes.'

These words fell loudly on the ears of Simba, the lion, who lay unseen in the tall grass not two giraffe-lengths from him; while Boohoo, the hippo, snoozing in the water lily pond, thought, '*Mmm* – I'm not at all sure about that.'

Crow also heard this boasting and flew off to report it to Chewi.

Riff-raff moved to a suitably-sized umbrella tree. He pushed his head through the top and began to nibble the most succulent green shoots. So safe did he feel and so impressed was he by the sound of his own voice murmuring, 'I am hidden from the eyes of the jungle,' that he failed to notice the yellow and brown shadow that glided through the thornbush.

Simba, the lion, saw Leopard moving swiftly, silently forward, his eyes fixed on a head that stuck out from the top of the umbrella tree. Chewi crept closer. His mind kept telling him how well giraffe meat suited his stomach. Riff-raff kept nibbling, his mind dulled by a false sense of security.

Suddenly Chewi sprang. There was a crashing in the umbrella tree and then a long, uneasy silence. High overhead, vultures circled expectantly. Boohoo blinked his eyes sadly. '*Um* – what a pity he didn't have more sense.' He did not attempt to go to sleep again.

Chewi lay basking in the sun on a great brown rock. His stomach was most comfortably full, his mind at rest. Crow had told him of Chameleon's downfall. He mused, 'There was small wisdom in Lwivi saying, "I can hide from the eyes of Giraffe." He was almost as unwise as the giraffe who boasted that he was hidden from me.'

A satisfying, gurgling sound came from Leopard's interior. As he licked his forepaws he looked with satisfaction at his own spots, stretching his rippling muscles and noting how similar his spots were to the mottling of the sunlight and the rocks. He growled deeply in his throat as his thoughts went to the houses of men and those who hunted in the jungle with spear and bow and arrow. Then he relaxed and said in his mind, 'But I am safe. My nose is the sharpest in the whole jungle and my ears tell me more than those of any other animal. By my spots I am better hidden than any other creature.' He drew back his lips in a snarl that showed his splendid teeth and dug his long sharp claws into the ground. He rolled over on his side and stretched. 'Behold, I am more of a danger to the two-legged ones than they are to me.'

Hippo moved his great head. His half-closed eyes had been watching Mshale, the hunter, patiently crouched amongst the roots of the *buyu* tree. He saw Leopard yawn a great yawn while Mshale fitted an arrow to his bow and shot it with deadly accuracy.

Boohoo lumbered out of the pond and wandered down to the great river murmuring to himself, '*Um* – what should a hippo learn from today's happenings?' He thought how Chameleon could not hide from Giraffe. Giraffe could not hide from Leopard and Leopard could not hide from the hunter. He looked up at the many vultures who were now circling above. Many had already perched in the umbrella tree. Boohoo launched himself into the cool waters of the river and said, '*Mmmm*, truly, many eyes see those who feel safely hidden.' He could see Mshale walking home to his village with the leopard skin over his shoulder.

Mshale himself had been standing in the further shadows of the campfire as Daudi told the story. He got up and started to walk away as the story finished but he heard Daudi say, 'The words of Jesus himself are, "There is nothing covered that will not be revealed and hidden that will not be known".'

From the darkness came Mshale's voice, loud in the quietness of the night, 'How will God do these things? If I wish I can hide my thoughts because my face is smooth and free from anger and fear; surely I can hide from God.'

Those that listened said no words. None were necessary.

* * *

What's Inside the Fable?

Special Message: You cannot hide from God.

Adam and Eve tried. *Genesis chapter 3 verses 8 to 13.*

Jonah tried. *Read the book of Jonah.*

Psalm 139 is a poem which says the same thing. You may try to hide from God. But it never works.

6
TOTO CROSSES THE EQUATOR

Mgogo had set the campfire. He went to meet Daudi.

'Bwana, my heart has great uncertainty. I feel no different. I feel just the way I did before I asked Jesus to take away my sin and to forgive me.'

'So feelings are your problem?' smiled Daudi. 'Then you haven't heard of Toto's safari to the equator?'

'Not yet,' said Mgogo, as he and the others settled down to listen.

Toto, the monkey, was visiting his relations who lived in a place in the deep jungle where the trees were tall and leaves were very green and butterflies hovered over the water lilies. He came to an extremely large

buyu tree. Underneath it was a notice-board beside the road which read: EQUATOR.

He wondered what it said and then he saw Twiga, the giraffe, and Boohoo, the hippopotamus, coming towards him.

Twiga said, 'This is a very interesting place, Little Monkey.'

'*Um* – yes,' mumbled Boohoo, 'it's the middle of the world.'

Toto's eyes were full of excitement. 'The very middle?'

Twiga nodded. 'Yes. They call it the equator. Sit where you are in the *buyu* tree and you're in the southern hemisphere, but if you walk down that long limb and jump into the *kuyu* tree – then you'll be in the northern hemisphere. You will have crossed the equator.'

Toto scratched his head. This was a difficult thing for monkeys to understand. He had heard much about the north and the wonderful things that were there. Thoughts swirled round in his brain. He wanted to go that way and here he was only a few steps away. All he had to do was to jump and he'd be there. He wondered what it would feel like to be in the north. Exciting little tingles started between his ears and scampered right down to the tip of his tail. He walked up and down the limb, talking softly to himself and thinking how different he would soon feel. How greatly he wanted to feel different.

From the shadows came a voice, a soft sugary, hissy sort of voice, 'It will be wonderful, Little Monkey. Keep thinking how different it's all going to feel. You will know you're there because you will be full of a wonderful joy.'

Giraffe and Hippo who were standing in the shade, listened and watched anxiously. A dreamy look came into little monkey's eyes.

'Careful,' called Twiga. 'That's Nzoka, the snake. He knows you've decided to cross the equator so now he wants to try and spoil it for you.'

'*Um* – don't take any notice of the cunning of snakes. There's poison in the things he's telling you.'

'Boohoo's right,' agreed Twiga. 'The north's the place. It's Elephant country. When you're close to him you're safe. It's the place of real happiness if you trust him.'

Toto turned away from Snake. He looked at Twiga and Boohoo and thought of Elephant and he decided what he would do. At once he ran along the limb shouting, 'I'm going north!' He jumped far out and landed safely on a limb of the *kuyu* tree but he felt no bump as he crossed the equator. He crouched in the *kuyu* tree quivering with excitement. He'd done it! He was in the north! Old things were behind. Everything would be different now. He waited for it to happen. But he felt the same – exactly the same.

The same wind blew on him. The same sun shone down. Had he really crossed over that line? From down below under the *kuyu* tree came Snake's voice very coaxingly, 'They're deceiving you, little friend.

54

Come down here. I know the path you want. Thrills. Excitement. Adventure. Tingling feelings. Doing things and not being found out. You'll feel wonderful if you go my way.' The enticing voice seemed to draw him down then he saw Boohoo and Twiga looking up at him.

'*Um*, Toto,' came Hippo's voice. 'Don't forget the day when you looked into Snake's eyes.'

Little Monkey thought of that terrible day when he *had* looked into Snake's eyes and had nearly become Snake's dinner. He heard Giraffe's voice, kindly and close to him, 'Toto, you may not feel different at once but use your eyes. You're now in the *kuyu* tree and the *kuyu* tree *is* in the northern hemisphere. Geography is geography.'

Toto nodded doubtfully but his mind still felt dizzy. 'Twiga, surely I should feel different if this north is what you say it is.' He sat on a wide piece of the limb. He read the EQUATOR notice spelling it forwards and backwards. He read it by hanging by his arms and hanging by his tail. It said the same thing every time. He felt the *kuyu* tree firm beneath his paws. 'Surely,' he said out loud, 'surely it is true. I am in the northern hemisphere. But I don't feel any different.'

Twiga's head was close to him. 'Facts are facts, Little Monkey. A *kuyu* tree is a *kuyu* tree.'

'*Um* – yes,' agreed Boohoo. '*Er* – why don't you continue in a northerly direction?'

'He's right,' nodded Twiga. 'The further you go, the more you will know where you are and where you are going, and the more you will feel it.'

'Yes,' said Boohoo firmly. 'Didn't Elephant say, the further you go, the better you'll know?'

Toto took their advice and the way things turned out he was so glad that he had.

Daudi smiled at all those who listened. But Mgogo knew that he was talking particularly to him. 'When we believe in Jesus and ask him to be our Saviour, our faces look the same, our voices sound the same and our bodies feel the same but we are different deep inside. We have become one of God's children. Our sins are forgiven. We have new life that will never end. We know this is true because God says it is so and we trust him – we have faith in him. This is what matters – not feelings.'

* * *

What's Inside the Fable?

Special Message: Don't be tripped by *feelings*.

1 Kings chapter 19 verses 2 to 21 tell about the prophet and the wicked queen.

Job – a whole book about a man and his feelings. He had a terrible time but he said, 'I KNOW that my redeemer lives.' *Job chapter 19 verses 25 and 26.*

7

MONKEYS FIND SOLID SAFETY

Mgogo looked worried, 'Bwana Daudi, are you quite sure that God gives everlasting life to the people who ask to be forgiven?'

Daudi nodded. 'Quite sure.'

'I wish I could feel it inside me. I hope it happened but ...'

'Tali and Kali had the same problem,' smiled Daudi.

The limbs of the *kuyu* tree stretched far out over the treacherous mud of the swamp called *Matope*. From the limbs of this great tree dangled long, thick, rope-like vines.

Again and again Nyani had warned the monkeys of his family tree not to go near the swamp. In a voice that trembled he would say, 'It was there we lost your cousin, Koko. It is a place of no joy where danger lurks – danger greater than the teeth of crocodiles.'

His words, however, had not taken root in the minds of Tali and Kali, the monkey twins. Chattering cheerfully, they climbed the *kuyu* tree and scampered down a broad limb, nearly upsetting Lwivi, the chameleon. They slid down a great trailing creeper and swung far out over the mud and then back almost to the bank.

Lwivi walked jerkily down the limb and stopped where the vine twisted over the branch. Chameleon's unblinking eye noticed that with each swing some of the vine fibres parted at the spot where Gwili, the millipede, used to sharpen his teeth.

Along the bank strolled Boohoo, the hippopotamus. He kept well away from the edge of the swamp. Seeing the monkeys he called out, '*Um* – enjoy yourselves, little fellows, but don't fall in. *Um-* even hippos won't have anything to do with that sticky sort of mud because ...'

The little monkeys giggled and gurgled as their swinging stirred up the hot steamy air above the swamp. Boohoo stopped in a patch of shade and nodded to Tembo, the elephant, and Twiga, the giraffe, as they came down to a place where clear water bubbled out beneath a great rock.

Up in the *kuyu* tree Chameleon was worried to see that the further the monkeys swung and the more often they did it, fibre after fibre of the creeper gave way. But Boohoo was complaining so loudly about the heat that the monkey twins could not hear what Lwivi was trying to tell them. Yelling with excitement they swung towards the bank and passed just over Twiga's head. Then back went the vine – far out over the swamp. Chameleon backed away as he saw the last small strands of the vine stretch dangerously.

Tembo and Twiga heard a tearing noise as it snapped and head over tail the twins tumbled into the swamp and were gripped by the glue-like mud.

'Help!' they screamed. 'Help!'

'Oh dear,' boomed Boohoo. 'That's one place where I can do nothing to help. Get into that mud and it's the end of any hippo. *Um* – I'm afraid nobody can do anything for them.'

But Tembo, the elephant, came to the edge of the rock that at one place lay above the level of the swamp. He put all his weight on it. It was firm. He trumpeted, 'Tali and Kali, don't struggle. Try to lie flat. Don't struggle. You can't get out by yourselves. Keep your eyes on us.' He spoke urgently to Twiga who moved to the edge of the rock. Tembo stood behind him and took a grip on his tail.

Giraffe leant forward, his knees bent, his neck stretched out at full length. He would have slipped into the mud but for Elepant. Lower and lower went his head till his chin was almost in the slime. Four monkey arms stretched up and clutched at his neck. There was a struggle but at last they had a firm grip.

'Oh – *um* – good,' said Hippo. '*Er*, carefully, now.' But the mud was terribly strong. It clung to them. It seemed to be dragging them down. Tali and Kali whimpered with fear. Hippo's eyes stuck out. 'Twiga, be careful. Be careful. Don't fall in yourself. We don't want – *um* ...'

Slowy two miserable little creatures were eased out of the swamp. They dripped thick, evil-smelling mud as Giraffe gently lowered them onto the rock. Trembling and shocked they sat clasping each other.

'Th-thank you, Twiga,' they stammered.

'Er, Twiga couldn't have reached you if Tembo hadn't – *um* ...'

Elephant's big kind voice asked, 'Are you safe, Small Monkeys?'

They looked bewildered. 'W-w-we're not sure.'

'Move over here into the sun – into the middle of this rock,' advised Twiga.

Clinging together they did so. Again Elephant spoke. 'Put all your feet on to the ground. Do they sink? Is the rock solid?'

'I hope so,' muttered Kali.

Tembo looked at Twiga with a twinkle in his eye and said patiently, 'Hard. Put those feet down *hard* and use your tails as well. Go on. Both of you. Look

at what they grip. Is mud like that? Now try to sink. Try with all your strength.'

Little monkeys smiled at each other. 'It's solid. We *are* safe.'

'True,' said Twiga. 'You are safe indeed. The rock won't let you sink. It's not a matter of hoping that you're safe. You can be sure.'

Daudi leaned back. 'It's wonderful to be sure, to be certain. Jesus is like that rock. You're safe when you put your trust firmly in him.

'The words of the Bible are, "You are my rock and my fortress. You are my hope, O Lord. You are my strong refuge".'

Mgogo was one of the last to go. He said quietly to Daudi, 'I understand now, and it is a thing of great comfort. Surely there is safety for your soul when your feet are on the ground and that rock is Jesus.'

* * *

What's Inside the Fable?

Special Message: Jesus is utterly dependable.

Read *1 John chapter 5 verses 10 to 13* and Jesus' own words to you in *John chapter 5 verse 24 and chapter 6 verses 39 and 40.*

Poetry – *Psalm 31 verses 1 to 5 and Psalm 62 verses 1 and 2.*

8
FAMOUS MONKEY LAST WORDS

Daudi put his hand on Mgogo's shoulder. 'If you want your dog to be happy and also to have happiness in your dog, the secret is to teach him to obey. Not sometimes, not just when it suits him, but to obey all the time.

'This doesn't often work for monkeys – some learn to obey and some don't. Nyani and Twiga tried hard.'

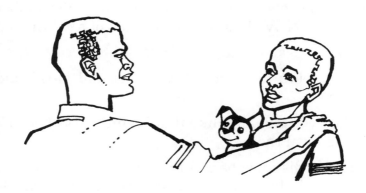

Toto and his monkey uncle, Nyani, were turning over flat stones and feasting on scorpions and cockroaches. They had climbed a hill which stood out like a giant ant hill above the thornbush jungle. As they moved between the great granite boulders, carefully avoiding spiky cactuses, Nyani said, 'We monkeys need to be very watchful in places like this, for amongst these great stones often lurk our enemies, python and leopard. You must know the rules of the jungle and obey them and you'll be safe. Disobey them and you'll be in trouble.'

Toto nodded. 'I know the first one already. *If you smell a leopard, climb a tree and go far out on a thin limb.*'

'Well done,' said Nyani, catching a particularly large cockroach and giving it to Toto. 'And the second rule says, *"Don't stand at the back of a zebra".*' In alarm Nyani held up his paw. 'Did you hear that?'

They listened, and then saw Twiga, the giraffe, and Boohoo, the hippo, coming towards them. Twiga smiled. 'I'm glad you're learning the rules. Remember specially, NEVER stand at the back of a zebra.'

'Why?' asked Toto.

'If a zebra kicks you it will hurt and *hurt*,' said Twiga.

'And you wouldn't like that,' grunted Boohoo. '*Er* – look down there.'

In the distance beside the lake was Stripey, the zebra, quietly drinking ... and tip-toeing towards

him with a thornbush branch in his paws was Tuffi, Toto's cousin, who loved teasing people.

'Oh,' said Toto. 'And Tuffi knows the second rule: Don't stand at the back of a zebra."

At the top of his voice Boohoo bellowed. 'Tuffi. Stop it!'

But Little Monkey took no notice. He crept closer and stuck the thorns into the stripes just beside zebra's tail. They heard Tuffi's shout of laughter which stopped suddenly as two flying hooves hit him WHACK! He sailed through the air and landed with a sickening PLOP.

Nyani put his paws over his ears.

'You see,' said Twiga, 'why it's wise to keep the rules of the jungle. Disobey them and you'll be in trouble.'

They watched vultures swoop down from the clouds.

Toto stood very close to his monkey uncle and said, 'You were right. It does not pay to disobey.'

Nyani nodded, 'Let's go over the rules again. *If you smell a leopard, climb a tree and go far out on a thin limb. Don't stand at the back of a zebra and never, never look into a snake's eyes.*'

Over and over again Toto murmured the rules, getting them firmly into his monkey mind. It was just before sunset that he was so glad that he had. Twiga suddenly lifted his head up.

'What does your nose tell you?'

Boohoo blinked. '*Er* – nothing much. Only that leopard's about somewhere – *Ooooh*, leopard!'

Monkey nose told the same news. Nyani and Toto raced to the slenderest of the branches of the *buyu* tree, clinging with tails and paws. Chewi sprang

nimbly up the tree and climbed higher and higher, his fangs bared. How he loved monkey for dinner!

'Hold tight, Toto,' barked Nyani from his safe limb in the *buyu* tree. 'You have been wise. No leopard can climb the slender branches to which you and I cling.'

Leopard snarled horribly and growled deep in his throat to frighten Toto and shake him off the limb. Nyani's voice was full of encouragement. 'Stay where you are, Toto, and all will be well. His words have neither teeth nor claws.' Nyani made faces at the great spotted jungle cat and pelted him with buyu

fruit. 'It pays to obey,' he barked, as at long last Chewi, snarling, climbed down and slunk away into the jungle.

Next morning they were back amongst the great granite rocks chasing cockroaches. Nyani was scratching quietly in the shade when Twiga shouted a warning. 'Nyani, quickly. Toto's in trouble.' Monkey uncle leapt onto the top of the highest boulder and looked down. Below him on a smooth rock cowered a small grey monkey. Towards him slithered a great python, its head swaying. Nyani could hear the soft hiss, 'Look into my eyes, Toto. Gaze into them. You feel so sleepy.'

Little monkey yawned. 'Shut your eyes and sleep now.'

High above them, Nyani tugged and pulled at a big boulder with all his monkey might. It rocked. It moved. He heaved again. It skidded forward, rolled over and crashed into a thousand pieces just in front of a snake's head. The great reptile drew back and in that split second Nyani sprang, grabbed little monkey by the tail and barking with triumph leapt to a high limb in the nearest tree.

'He won't hurt you there,' mumbled Hippo. 'Snakes may bite …' He opened his great mouth. 'But so can hippos!'

They watched the python slide away into the dark places between the rocks. 'Snake nearly had you for his dinner,' said Twiga. 'You looked into his eyes.'

'He seemed so friendly,' muttered Toto.

'Was he, though?' asked Boohoo. 'You'll never forget the third rule of the jungle now.'

'Toto, it's good to know the rules. But it's not enough only to know them,' said Twiga.

Toto thought for a moment then he asked, 'And have I not also been taught that it pays to obey?'

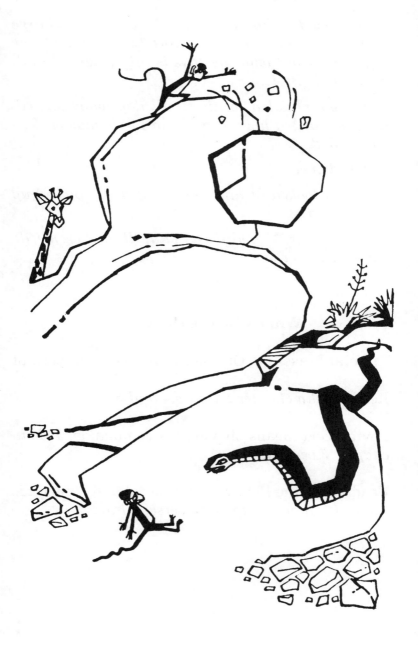

'Everybody who has asked Jesus to take charge of their lives knows that obeying him makes all the difference. And what he says is all in here.' Daudi held up his Bible.

Mgogo whistled to his small dog who stopped, turned, wagged his tail and ran to his master. The boy smiled.

'Obedience ...?'

Daudi looked at him and nodded. He picked up the small dog.

'Remember, Mgogo, Jesus said, "If you love me, do what I tell you".'

* * *

What's Inside the Fable?

Special Message: Obedience to God is all-important

Read *1 John chapter 2 verses 4 and 5.*

Loving God means obeying his commands. *1 John chapter 5 verse 3.*

Read about the king who disobeyed and ruined his life in *1 Samuel chapter 15 verses 11 to 26.*

9

THE MEDICALLY-MINDED MONKEY

Daudi was unusually quiet as he sat looking into the campfire. He threw a handful of dry leaves into the glowing coals and said, 'Let's think of the things that matter most. You know the word priorities – *the most important things?'*

There was a nodding of heads and Daudi started.

Pilli was a medium-sized monkey who loved to use long words. His favourite possession was a box labelled FIRST AID KIT and a book called *Medicines and First Aid for Monkeys and Others.*

Groggi was a thin monkey of small strength and strong sickness. He had great strength in his cough and small usefulness in his legs. He sat miserably propped against a *buyu* tree root, sadly listening to his Uncle Nyani telling a treeful of monkeys of the medical adventures and activity of Pilli, the medically-minded monkey. He told how cleverly Pilli could make simple things sound complicated and of his skill in tying things up with many sorts of bandages.

Silence came suddenly. Groggi opened his eyes a little and saw a serious-faced monkey holding a book and looking closely at his thin leg. In between coughing he thought, 'This must be, Pilli. Perhaps he can help me.' He watched him turn over page after page, frown and then slowly nod his head.

'*Mmmm*,' mused Pilli wisely. Then, '*Ah*.'

Groggi shivered and held onto his thin ribs for they gave him misery every time he coughed. 'Ah,' said Pilli again, opening his first aid box and taking out a rolled-up bandage with which he started to bind up Groggi's leg in the exact way that his book described.

Into the shade of the buyu tree strolled Twiga, the giraffe, Boohoo, the hippo, and Stripey, the zebra. They stopped to watch. Pilli glared peevishly at Groggi. 'I wish you wouldn't cough like that. It interferes with my activity.'

'I wish I didn't cough like this,' panted Groggi, clutching his ribs. 'Is there nothing in your box for coughs?'

Pilli looked at him scornfully and went on with his bandaging. There was perspiration on Groggi's brow and his teeth chattered with shivering. Pilli glared at him again. 'I wish you wouldn't shiver like that. It complicates my work.'

Groggi held his head in his hands and moaned. 'I wish I didn't shiver like this. I wish I didn't shiver like this. Is there nothing in your medical box for those that shiver?'

Medically-minded Monkey looked at him coldly. 'Do you or do you not want my assistance?'

Groggi was coughing too hard to answer.

Twiga bent his long neck down and asked gently, 'Can nothing be done for his cough?'

Pilli answered in a superior voice, 'Can shivering be splinted, or a cough bandaged?' He finished his work on Groggi and was about to close his first aid box when Stripey winked at Twiga and said, 'I have a pain in the last half of my tail. Can you be of any assistance?'

Pilli held up his paw. 'That undoubtedly calls for immobilisation.'

Zebra kicked up his heels, brayed like his distant relation, the donkey, and demanded, 'Calls for what?'

Pilli sighed. 'It must be kept from moving. A wide bandage and a safety pin is the answer.'

Stripey grinned a wide-toothed grin, pushed his

head close to Monkey and giggled, 'And what would I do about the flies?'

'That,' said Pilli loftily, 'is your problem. And I, too, find myself at a disadvantage. One of the special rules of monkey procedure is never stand behind the heels of a zebra.'

Boohoo nodded. 'and quite right too. I remember a little monkey who ... But he was very different from you, Pilli. Perhaps, however, you can help me because every time I sniff these little round yellow flowers that grow in thorn trees it gives me a great deal of ...'

'Discomfort,' said Pilli decidedly. 'I'll explain it to you. Now open your mouth wide and say *Aaah.*' He peered into the crimson cavern which was Hippo's mouth. He was interested to see two huge hippo tonsils and a great spread of hippo throat, red as a sunset on a dusty day. Pilli took up his book and started to read the chapter headed 'Tonsils, Throats and Such.'

Slowly Boohoo closed his mouth, blinked and watched. After a time Pilli nodded. '*Ah*, yes. Inflammation of the larynx and pharynx with obstruction of the nasal passages.' Bewildered Boohoo shut his eyes tight, but Twiga whispered, 'He means your throat is sore and your nose is blocked.'

Hippo smiled. '*Um* – yes. I'll show you what happens.'

He went over to a thorn tree and sniffed a tuft of acacia flowers. Then he stood absolutely still, his eyes wide open and tears started trickling down each side of his large face. '*Um* – it always happens like this.' He sniffed the flowers again.

Pilli was greatly interested. He came closer, his book under one arm and his box under the other. Hippo started making snorty noises. His nostrils quivered and then, unexpectedly he opened his mouth and sneezed mightily.

'*Hipposhoo!*' The force of that sneeze knocked Pilli onto his back. His book went one way and his box flew open, scattering pins, plaster, bandages, gauze and cotton wool all over the place. In a huff Pilli picked them up, crammed the box and strode off to his special *buyu* tree.

That night the jungle was disturbed by the sounds of Hippo sneezing and his loud complaining voice. Twiga heard him muttering, '*Er – um –* I'm not at all sure that even the largest bandage would help my, *um ...*' Sneeze after sneeze shook that part of the jungle and then a sad voice announced, 'And dow by dose is blogged. Oh dear.'

When Pilli came next morning to bandage Groggi's legs he took no notice of the strange wheezy noises that sick monkey made and he didn't seem even to notice his harsh, hacking cough. Boohoo came lumbering up from the river and stood in front of Pilli. '*Um –* I didn't sleep a wink all night. Sneezing, wheezing, and itching. Most uncomfortable. Have you something in your box that will, *um ...*'

Pilli nodded briskly, and taking a large triangular bandage, tied it firmly round Hippo's head just above his nostrils. The loose corner flapped every time Boohoo breathed. His little ears twitched. He rolled his eyes, made gulpy noises and sneezed violently.

The bandage was torn to ribbons. Boohoo sat down with his back against an ant hill and tried to press on his upper lip with his left foot. When the sneezes had quietened he mumbled, 'I don't think bandages do much good for sneezes.' He looked sadly across at Groggi.

Pilli had already started to put bandages on his very thin legs. Hippo watched and then he asked, 'Are you sure that bandages are the answer to our troubles?'

Medically-minded Monkey said nothing, but the way he curled up his tail and the corners of his mouth left no doubt as to what he thought of the intelligence of hippos.

That evening he came back and inspected his handiwork, tightening the bandage here and loosening it there. Then he stood back with his head on one side. Twiga came up behind him and bent his long neck down. All day long he had felt alarm growing within him as he listened to the coughing of sick monkey. He said softly, 'Is it not more important to treat the inner troubles of your relation? The matter of greatest importance is surely his life, not his legs?'

But Pilli tilted his nose up in a superior way and said, 'I will not allow outside interference when I am treating a patient.'

Next day when he arrived with a paw full of bandages he found a group of serious-faced monkeys standing sorrowfully at the foot of the family tree. They broke the sad news. 'Groggi is no more.'

Medically-minded Monkey's nose twitched with anger. 'This cannot be so,' he announced. 'I bandaged his legs daily with considerable skill.'

Boohoo shook his head sadly and Twiga murmured to him, 'Might it be that bandaging legs is not the best treatment for troubles in the chest?'

Again there was silence. Drums beat in the distance of that warm African night.

'Priorities,' said Daudi suddenly. 'Things that matter most. Think of these things carefully. A man's place on earth has small value compared with his place in heaven. Compare the size of Mouse with that of Elephant. So is life on earth compared to eternal life. Your body is much less important than your soul.'

He threw more leaves on the fire and read from his Bible the words of Jesus, 'Seek first the kingdom of God and righteousness.'

* * *

What's Inside the Fable?

Special Message: Put God *first* in your life.

Read what Jesus said: *Matthew chapter 6 verses 19 to 34 and chapter 22 verses 34 to 40.*

The Old Testament says the same thing in *Deuteronomy chapter 5 verses 1 to 22 and chapter 11 verses 1 to 26.*

GLOSSARY

JUNGLE DOCTOR'S WORDS AND NAMES
How to say them and what they mean

Animals	*Pronunciation*
Boko - monkey	Boekoe
Boohoo - hippo	Boohoo
Chewi - leopard	Chewee
Chibwa - dog	Cheebwer
Groggi - monkey	Grogee
Gwili - millipede	Gweelee
Kali - monkey twin	Karlee
Koko - monkey	Cocoa
Kookoo - hen	Kookoo
Lwivi -chameleon	Lweevee
Mbisi - hyena	Mbeesee
Mbuzi - goat	Mboozee
Moto - monkey	Mowtoe
Nyani - monkey	Nyahnee
Nzoka - snake	Nzoker
Pilli - monkey	Pillee
Riff-raff - Twiga's nephew	Riff-raff
Simba - lion	Simber
Slinki - jackal	Slinkee
Sticki - monkey	Stickee
Stripey - zebra	Stripey
Suku - parrot	Sookoo
Tabu - monkey	Taboo
Tali - monkey twin	Tarlee
Tembo - elephant	Temboe
Toto - monkey twin	Toetoe
Tuffi - Toto's cousin	Tuffee
Tumbo - monkey	Toomboe
Twiga - giraffe	Twigger
Vibi - vulture	Veebee
Waa - hornbill	Wah

Names	Pronunciation	English
Chuma	Choomer	Leopard hunter
Daudi	Dhawdee	David
Mboga	Mbowger	Vegetable
Mdimi	Mdeemee	Shepherd
Mgogo	Mmgogoe	
Mshale	Mshalay	Arrow, hunter

Swahili	Pronunciation	English
Asante	Asarntay	Thank you
Buyu	Booyoo	Baobab tree
Bwana	Bwarner	Sir, Mister, Lord
Dudu	Doodoo	Insect
Eheh	Ayhay	Agreement (with nod of head)
Hongo	Hongo!	Behold*
Kah	Kah	Exclamation*
Kali	Karlee	Fierce
Matope	Martoepay	Mud
Muwaha	Moowahar	Important person
Panga	Parnger	Jungle knife
Yoh	Yoe	Exclamation (please raise the eyebrows)

*(tone of voice will indicate amazement, surprise or disgust)

3

TABU TRUSTS

Daudi had a bag in his hand. He opened it and produced two large ripe mangoes. 'Food for those that listen,' he laughed.

'Asante, Bwana Daudi,' chorused Mgogo and Goha.

'Before you eat them, listen to my story for in it there is food for your soul.'

Tabu sat on a branch of the thorny acacia tree and laughed as he shook it as hard as he could. Down showered juicy seed pods. Underneath were a whole family of gazelle. They eagerly gobbled up their favourite food.

'You're stupid, Tabu,' yelled Sticki, the sweet-toothed monkey. 'Stop jumping about. Grab those juicy beauties with your paws and eat them yourself.' He looked over his shoulder. Out of the tall grass came Tembo, the elephant. Sticki hastily swung off through the jungle.

With great friendliness the strongest animal in the jungle stretched out his trunk. 'Hullo, Tabu. Why don't you do what Sticki said?'

Tabu jumped down onto Tembo's back and then onto his tusk. 'You said to love others as much as I love myself. You said to do for others what you'd like them to do for you.'

Elephant coiled up the end of his trunk. Tabu slid into the strong comfortable seat. He was happier than he had ever been. 'Thank you, Tembo, for saving me from the trap and rescuing me from the river. And thank you for telling me the best way to do things.'

Tembo flapped his big ears. 'Use your ears, Tabu. When I tell you to do something do it fast. Don't wait to ask why?'

Tabu was going to ask why, but then he saw the friendship in Elephant's eye and and felt the strength of his trunk. He thought, 'It's terrifc to be able to trust Elephant.'

Later on, up the acacia tree, Waa and Suku came and perched on each side of him. Tabu was excited. He swung back and forth with his tail coiled round the limb and chuckled, 'There's no one like Tembo. I've learned something new today. When Tembo says do something I'll do it fast.'

Waa's deep voice came, 'Obey, without delay.'

Tabu nodded, 'I like that. Obey without delay. It hasn't happened yet.'

Suku squawked, 'It will. And when it does don't cry why?'

Tabu chuckled, 'I like that too. Obey without delay and don't cry why?'

He shook down more seed pods and had a game with the gazelles and then sat on top of the ant hill and thought about Elephant and what he said. Behind him came a soft voice, 'You're a clever monkey.'

Tabu turned round quickly and saw Slinki smiling up at him slyly. He liked to be told that he was clever but he knew that Jackal never came near Elephant if he could help it and never did what he said.

Slinki kept on talking fast. 'I think that the way you swing by your tail is wonderful – just wonderful.'

Monkey scampered up the buyu tree and swung from a thin branch.

'Beautiful.' Jackal jumped up and down excitedly. 'Not far from here is an *mpunga* tree with long vines hanging down from its limbs. Wonderful thing to swing on.'

'No!' growled Tabu with his hands on his hips. 'No. I'm not going near that swamp.'

Slinki shook his head hard. 'It is not really at the swamp. It's just a little way downhill. You could swing wonderfully on those vines – better than anybody else. You're a top monkey, Tabu.'

Tabu hesitated.

Down the hill under the mpunga tree Crocodile hid in a narrow creek and watched. High in the air Vibi, the vulture, circled and watched.

Suku whispered to Waa, 'Something's going on. Crunch and his lot are up to something.'

Tabu thought how lovely it would feel to swing through the warm air. The bigger the swing the better it would feel. He scrambled down and said, 'Show me where the *mpunga* tree is, Slinki.' He couldn't help noticing Jackal's looks of admiration and he felt big when he said, 'You really are a top monkey.'

Jackal went on talking fast as they hurried down the slope – then he stopped and pointed, 'There it is. Look!'

'*Wow!*' chirped Tabu, his eyes gleaming. He looked at the long, strong vines. 'Thick as a monkey's tail. Wow! WOW! Just watch me.' He grabbed the thickest vine and swung up into the air. 'Top monkey is right, Slinki,' he yelled, going higher and higher.

'See how close you can get to the ground,' challenged Slinki as Monkey whizzed past him.

He saw a movement among the reeds and a yellow gloating eye gleamed and Crocodile's jaws opened hopefully. Monkey swung past again, his tail only a coconut's height from the ground.

'Well done,' shouted Slinki. 'See if you can brush the ground with the fur of your back this time.'

Waa flew fast through the branches. Nearby he saw Elephant. 'Help. Quickly. Tabu. The *mpunga* tree. Crocodile's hiding nearby.' He squawked in his excitement.

Silently Tembo raced down the hill

'This time,' Tabu shouted. 'I'll do it this time, Slinki. Watch.'

Crunch shuffled to a place where he could pounce open-mouthed and trap monkey in his jaws. 'One more swing and he's mine,' gloated Crocodile.

Monkey was halfway up that last swing when a great voice sounded through the jungle. 'Tabu, climb up high – NOW.' In a split second monkey realised it was Elephant. He shot up the vine to the very top. CRUNCH! There was a crashing of huge jaws. The lower half of the vine was in Crocodile's mouth. Yellow eyes flashed in fury.

Tabu struggled onto a strong limb. Elephant burst through the thorny scrub. Seeing him, Crocodile bolted for the deep dark pool.

Jackal cringed into a hollow log and Vibi flew high up into the heat haze.

Elephant stopped under the limb where Monkey clung shivering. Tabu jumped and clasped his arms round Elephant's tusk. 'Thank you, Tembo,' he panted. 'Thank you for being close.'

'Well done, little friend,' came the words down the trunk. 'You obeyed. You didn't wait to ask why?'

'*Ooooof*,' shuddered Tabu. 'Wouldn't that have been an awful mistake?' Inside his head he saw again those great jaws and those terrible teeth.

'Trust me and obey me,' said Elephant. 'That's the way to the life that really matters. We'll enjoy it together.'

Daudi took a mango in each hand and held them out to the boys. As they took them he put his hands in the air. 'It's with your hands that you do things. Your soul has two hands. They are called trust and obey. If you trust him then you obey him and Jesus said: 'If you love me keep my commandments – do what I tell you''.'

* * *

What's Inside the Fable?

Special Message: Trusting Jesus also means obeying him. If we have trusted Jesus we have crossed over from death to life. *John chapter 5 verse 24.*

Now if we love him, we must obey him. *John chapter 14 verses 23 and 24.*

JUNGLE DOCTOR'S ANIMAL STORIES

These classic stories have a magic all of their own. Above all, they are characterised by the hallmark of all great storytelling – they are a delight to six-year-olds as well as to those ten times that tender age.

Jungle Doctor's Fables
There was once a monkey who didn't believe in crocodiles – but that did not make any difference when he met one. Another monkey tried to pull himself out of a swamp by his whiskers - all that was left of him was two small bubbles on the top of the mud!
ISBN: 978-1-84550-608-7

Jungle Doctor's Monkey Tales
Small monkeys never could remember not to get too near to the hind feet of a zebra, nor to throw coconuts at Chewi, the leopard, nor to look into the eyes of snakes. Fortunately, Uncle Nyani, the sole survivor of a family of seven, is always there to do his best to knock some sense into their heads!
ISBN: 978-1-84550-609-4

Jungle Doctor's Tug-of-War
Even by monkey standards, Toto was pretty dim. The Jungle underworld, in the form of Crunch, the crocodile, Mbisi the hyena, Slinki the jackal, Vibi the vulture and Gnark, the crow think he will turn out to be easy meat.
ISBN: 978-1-84550-610-0

Jungle Doctor's Hippo Happenings

Boohoo, the Unhappy Hippo had a great deal of empty space between his strangely-shaped ears, and he suffered not only from hayfever, but from an equally frightful desire to help people, usually with unexpected results.

ISBN: 978-1-84550-611-7

Jungle Doctor's Rhino Rumblings

Rhino has small eyes, a big body, a tiny brain, and a huge idea of his own importance. But his adventures turn him into a rather different animal.

ISBN: 978-1-84550-612-4

Jungle Doctor meets Mongoose

Again and again the snake struck, but the flying ball of fur with the fiery eyes always managed to jump backwards – just out of range.

ISBN: 978-1-84550-613-1

CHRISTIAN FOCUS PUBLICATIONS

Christian
Focus

Christian
Heritage

CF4K

Mentor

Christian Focus Publications publishes books for adults and children under its four main imprints: Christian Focus, CF4K, Mentor and Christian Heritage. Our books reflect that God's word is reliable and Jesus is the way to know him, and live for ever with him.

Our children's publication list includes a Sunday School curriculum that covers pre-school to early teens; puzzle and activity books. We also publish personal and family devotional titles, biographies and inspirational stories that children will love.

If you are looking for quality Bible teaching for children then we have an excellent range of Bible story and age specific theological books.

From pre-school to teenage fiction, we have it covered!

Find us at our web page:
www.christianfocus.com

CF4∙K
Because you're never
too young to know Jesus